The NatureTrail Bo
INSECTWATCHING

Ruth Thomson

Identifying Insects with this Book

This is a book about common European insects you can find. It tells you about how they live, move, eat and grow, and also shows you where to find them. When you see an insect, and you want to know its name, or more about it, use this book as follows:

Turn to the back of the book (pages 28–31) and look it up in the section called **Common Insects to Spot.** If you can't see a picture of it there . . .

. . . turn to the pages which deal with the **kind of place** where you found it. For example, pages 14–15 tell you about pond insects.

If you still can't find it, look on other pages in the book, such as pages 18–19 which show you how different insects move, or pages 6–7 where there is a section called Differences to Spot. Always make careful notes about insects you find and try to identify them later.

Usborne Publishing

First published in 1976 by
Usborne Publishing Ltd,
20 Garrick Street,
London WC2

Bumble Bee

Peacock Butterfly

Written by
Ruth Thomson

Series Editor
Sue Jacquemier

Consultant Editor
Anthony Wootton

Designed by
Nick Eddison and
Sally Burrough

Illustrated by
John Barber, Stephen Bennett,
Roland Berry, Don Forrest, Chris
Howell-Jones, Colin King, Richard
Lewington, Phillip Richardson,
Jim Robins, David Watson, Phil
Weare, Adrian Williams, Roy
Wiltshire

Made and Printed in England by
Purnell & Sons Ltd.

Cardinal Beetle

**Large Marsh
Grasshopper**

Small Tortoiseshell
Butterfly

The NatureTrail Book of
INSECTWATCHING

About This Book

This book tells you where to look for common European insects. It shows you how insects live in different kinds of places, how to make notes and how to keep insects. Wherever possible, the insects have been drawn life size. Where lengths are given, they refer to the length of the insect from the tip of its abdomen to its head, not including the antennae. The sizes given for winged insects refer to their wing span (from wing-tip to wing-tip).

Contents

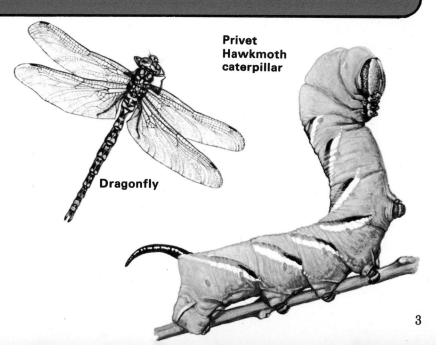

Dragonfly

Privet
Hawkmoth
caterpillar

Becoming an Insect Watcher

You can find insects almost anywhere, so it is easy to start watching them. Look first at as many kinds of insects as you can find so that you learn how they differ from other animals. Later you may want to study one or two kinds in more detail.

There are more *kinds* of insects (called *species*) than all the different kinds of mammals, fish, birds and reptiles put together. People are still discovering new species and finding out more about ones already known.

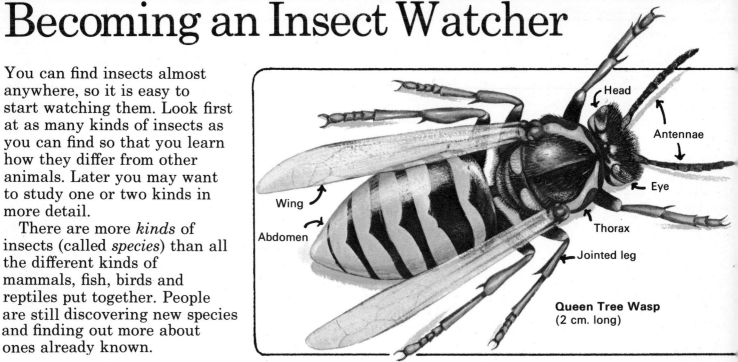

Head

Antennae

Eye

Thorax

Jointed leg

Wing

Abdomen

Queen Tree Wasp
(2 cm. long)

What You Need

These are some of the things it is useful to have if you want to be an insect-watcher. You will need a good pocket lens and a field notebook for recording what you see. Choose a lens which magnifies 8 or 10 times. It is a good idea to fix it on some string round your neck, to keep it handy. You may not need all the things shown: it depends on where you want to look for insects.

LAY A WHITE SHEET UNDER A BUSH. BEAT THE BUSH WITH A STICK. THE SHEET WILL CATCH FALLING INSECTS

A BUTTERFLY NET MAY BE USEFUL. STALK THE INSECT SLOWLY AND QUIETLY. TRY NOT TO HARM IT

A SMALL TROWEL IS USEFUL FOR DIGGING UP EARTH. SIEVE THE SOIL TO FIND INSECTS

Quick Sketches

Make quick sketches of the insects you find. When you get home, look them up and try to identify them.

1 Draw three ovals for the head, thorax and abdomen.

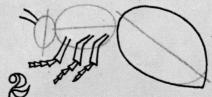

2 Draw the insect's legs and antennae in position.

3 Draw in the wings, if the insect has any.

4

Add any special markings or colours if you have time.

What is an Insect?

All adult insects have three parts to their bodies: a head, a thorax (middle) and an abdomen (lower part). On their heads they have a pair of antennae, used mainly for smelling and feeling. Most insects have a pair of large eyes and all insects have three pairs of jointed legs (at some time in their lives) attached to the thorax. Most adult insects have wings. Apart from birds and bats, insects are the only other kind of animals that can fly properly.

These are not Insects

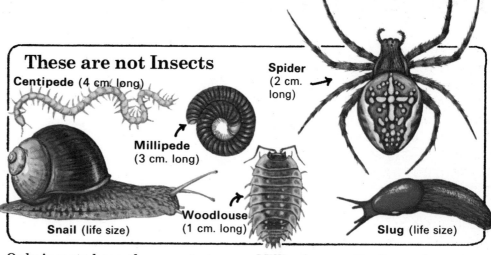

Centipede (4 cm. long)

Millipede (3 cm. long)

Snail (life size)

Woodlouse (1 cm. long)

Spider (2 cm. long)

Slug (life size)

Only insects have three parts to their body and three pairs of legs. Slugs and snails have no legs at all, and spiders have eight legs.

Millipedes, centipedes and woodlice have bodies made up of lots of parts, called segments, and have legs on every segment.

THE MOST IMPORTANT THING YOU NEED IS A NOTEBOOK. USE A NEW PAGE FOR EACH INSECT YOU FIND

YOU COULD MARK OFF AN AREA WITH STRING AND SEE HOW MANY INSECTS YOU FIND THERE

TAKE A BAG WITH POCKETS TO CARRY YOUR EQUIPMENT IN

CARRY INSECTS IN SCREW-TOP JARS OR BOXES LINED WITH PAPER OR MOSS

July 13th Heron Meadow 2pm Sunny

Cinnabar Caterpillars on leaves and stem of Ragwort. Colour-Yellow and black stripes.

HERON MEADOW gate

Cinnabar Caterpillars on Ragwort

bush

Ants' nest under stones

Keeping a Notebook

It is best to use a spiral-bound notebook for your notes. Then you can tear off pages and keep together all the notes you gather at different times on a particular insect. Make rough notes while you are watching; you can always make more careful ones later. Write down the date and the time when you saw the insect and what the weather was like. Try to describe the insect and the plant you found it on as fully as possible. If you find something that you want to look at again, make a map of where you found it.

Differences to Spot

QUICK CHECK LIST

WHEN YOU FIND AN INSECT, LOOK FIRST TO SEE WHETHER IT HAS WINGS AND, IF SO, HOW MANY.

IF IT HAS ONE PAIR OF WINGS, LOOK AT CHART A.

IF IT HAS TWO PAIRS OF WINGS, LOOK AT CHART B.

IF IT HAS NO WINGS, LOOK AT CHART C.

IF IT HAS HARD WING-CASES, LOOK AT CHART D.

It is not always easy to tell one insect from another. Some Flies look very like Bees, while many Bugs look like Beetles. There are many different species of insects—perhaps a million in the world. Only a few are shown here—turn to pages 28–31 to see more.

When you are taking notes on an insect you have found, try to make a habit of asking yourself several questions about it. Does it have wings? How many pairs? Does the insect have hard wing-cases? The charts on this page show some of the insects which have these features.

This is not a scientific method of classifying insects, but it will help you to group them in your own mind. Take notes on anything else that you notice about the insect. Does it have antennae? How long are they? Does the insect have legs, and if so, how many? Remember that insects change colour and shape as they grow into adults, and that the male of a species is sometimes a different colour from the female.

A Insects with One Pair of Wings

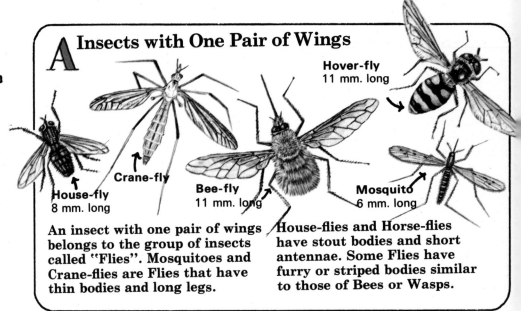

Hover-fly 11 mm. long

Crane-fly

House-fly 8 mm. long

Bee-fly 11 mm. long

Mosquito 6 mm. long

An insect with one pair of wings belongs to the group of insects called "Flies". Mosquitoes and Crane-flies are Flies that have thin bodies and long legs.

House-flies and Horse-flies have stout bodies and short antennae. Some Flies have furry or striped bodies similar to those of Bees or Wasps.

B Insects with Two Pairs of Wings

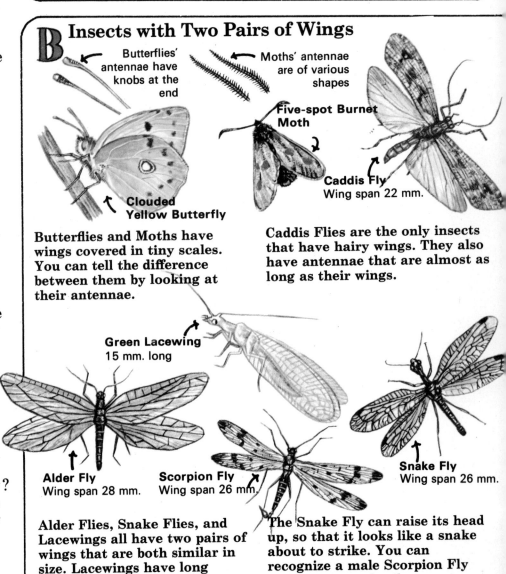

Butterflies' antennae have knobs at the end

Moths' antennae are of various shapes

Five-spot Burnet Moth

Caddis Fly Wing span 22 mm.

Clouded Yellow Butterfly

Butterflies and Moths have wings covered in tiny scales. You can tell the difference between them by looking at their antennae.

Caddis Flies are the only insects that have hairy wings. They also have antennae that are almost as long as their wings.

Green Lacewing 15 mm. long

Alder Fly Wing span 28 mm.

Scorpion Fly Wing span 26 mm.

Snake Fly Wing span 26 mm.

Alder Flies, Snake Flies, and Lacewings all have two pairs of wings that are both similar in size. Lacewings have long antennae and translucent wings.

The Snake Fly can raise its head up, so that it looks like a snake about to strike. You can recognize a male Scorpion Fly by its up-turned tail.

Where no size is given in a label, the insect is drawn life size.

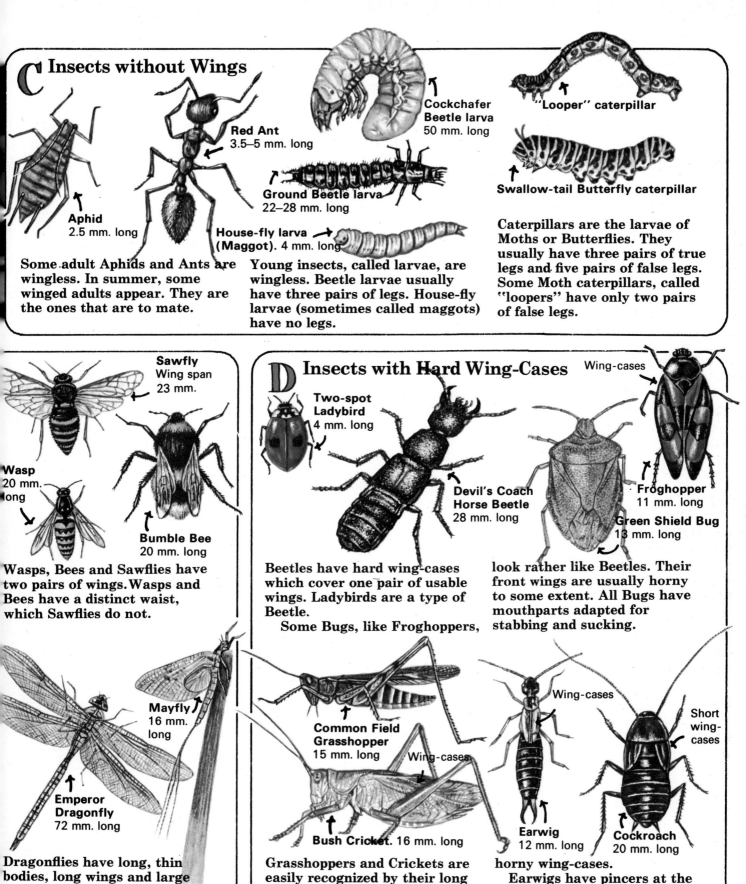

C Insects without Wings

Cockchafer Beetle larva 50 mm. long

"Looper" caterpillar

Red Ant 3.5–5 mm. long

Ground Beetle larva 22–28 mm. long

Swallow-tail Butterfly caterpillar

Aphid 2.5 mm. long

House-fly larva (Maggot). 4 mm. long

Some adult Aphids and Ants are wingless. In summer, some winged adults appear. They are the ones that are to mate.

Young insects, called larvae, are wingless. Beetle larvae usually have three pairs of legs. House-fly larvae (sometimes called maggots) have no legs.

Caterpillars are the larvae of Moths or Butterflies. They usually have three pairs of true legs and five pairs of false legs. Some Moth caterpillars, called "loopers" have only two pairs of false legs.

Sawfly Wing span 23 mm.

Wasp 20 mm. long

Bumble Bee 20 mm. long

Wasps, Bees and Sawflies have two pairs of wings. Wasps and Bees have a distinct waist, which Sawflies do not.

D Insects with Hard Wing-Cases

Wing-cases

Two-spot Ladybird 4 mm. long

Devil's Coach Horse Beetle 28 mm. long

Froghopper 11 mm. long

Green Shield Bug 13 mm. long

Beetles have hard wing-cases which cover one pair of usable wings. Ladybirds are a type of Beetle.

Some Bugs, like Froghoppers, look rather like Beetles. Their front wings are usually horny to some extent. All Bugs have mouthparts adapted for stabbing and sucking.

Mayfly 16 mm. long

Common Field Grasshopper 15 mm. long

Wing-cases

Wing-cases

Short wing-cases

Emperor Dragonfly 72 mm. long

Bush Cricket. 16 mm. long

Earwig 12 mm. long

Cockroach 20 mm. long

Dragonflies have long, thin bodies, long wings and large eyes. Mayflies have two or three long threads at the end of the abdomen and small hind wings.

Grasshoppers and Crickets are easily recognized by their long hind legs, which they use for jumping. Most of them have one pair of wings, covered with

horny wing-cases.
Earwigs have pincers at the end of their bodies and short wing-cases. Cockroaches have bristly legs and long antennae.

Breeding, Growing and Changing

Almost all insects grow from eggs. The eggs hatch into young insects. Before they become adults, young insects must go through different stages of growth. Some young insects change shape completely. Others just get bigger. The ones on this page do not change their shape very much, only their size. The ones on the opposite page go through a further very different stage of growth after they hatch, before they become adult insects.

All insects have a soft skin at first, but this hardens and then cannot stretch. As they grow, insects have to change their skin. This is called moulting. A new skin grows under the old one. The old skin splits and the insect wriggles out, covered in its new, larger skin. Once the insect has become adult, it does not grow any more.

Some insects, like Crickets, Earwigs, Grasshoppers and Bugs, hatch from the eggs looking like smaller versions of the adults. They have no wings when they

hatch. These young insects are called nymphs. They moult several times, growing each time. The wings appear as small wing buds. At the last moult, the wing buds expand into wings.

The young of other insects, like Butterflies, Moths, Beetles, Flies, Ants, Bees and Gnats are called larvae. When they hatch from the eggs, they do not look like the adults they will become. They moult several times as they grow.

When these larvae have grown to a certain size, they

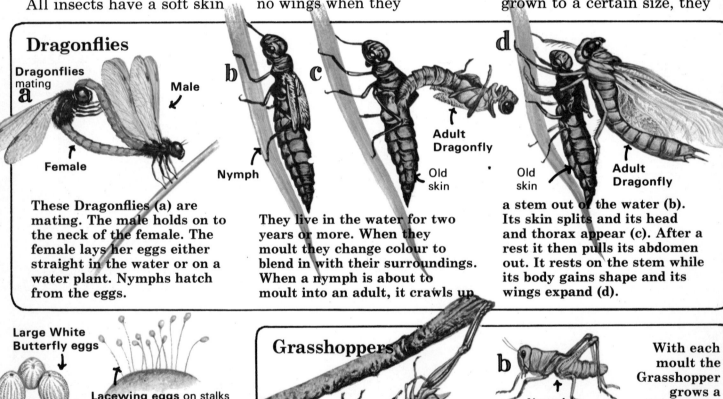

Dragonflies

Dragonflies mating
a

Male

Female

b

c

Nymph

Adult Dragonfly

Old skin

d

Old skin

Adult Dragonfly

These Dragonflies (a) are mating. The male holds on to the neck of the female. The female lays her eggs either straight in the water or on a water plant. Nymphs hatch from the eggs.

They live in the water for two years or more. When they moult they change colour to blend in with their surroundings. When a nymph is about to moult into an adult, it crawls up

a stem out of the water (b). Its skin splits and its head and thorax appear (c). After a rest it then pulls its abdomen out. It rests on the stem while its body gains shape and its wings expand (d).

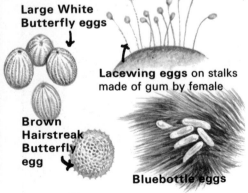

Large White Butterfly eggs

Lacewing eggs on stalks made of gum by female

Brown Hairstreak Butterfly egg

Bluebottle eggs

Female insects lay eggs, either singly or in clusters. A few insects, like the Earwig, look after their eggs and guard them, but most insects leave the eggs once they are laid.

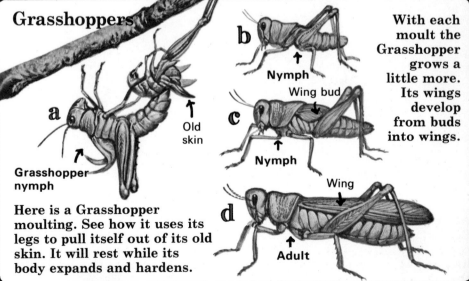

Grasshoppers

a

Old skin

Grasshopper nymph

Here is a Grasshopper moulting. See how it uses its legs to pull itself out of its old skin. It will rest while its body expands and hardens.

b

Nymph

c

Wing bud

Nymph

d

Wing

Adult

With each moult the Grasshopper grows a little more. Its wings develop from buds into wings.

shed their skin for the last time and become pupae. Pupae cannot feed and usually do not move. Inside the pupa, the body of the young insect changes into the adult insect.

When the adult is ready to emerge, the skin of the pupa splits and the adult struggles out. It does not grow any more after this.

The adult mates with an insect of the same species. Then the females look for places to lay their eggs. Some are laid on stems, some in or on the ground, and some in water.

Gnats

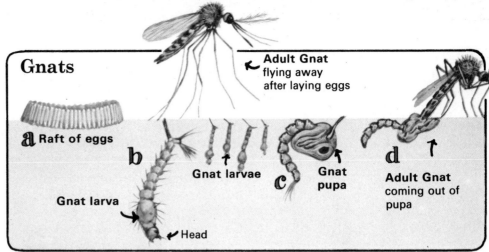

a Raft of eggs

b Gnat larva

Head

Gnat larvae

c Gnat pupa

d Adult Gnat coming out of pupa

Adult Gnat flying away after laying eggs

Gnats lay their eggs in groups, which float like a raft on the water's surface (a). The larvae (b) hatch out, and then hang from the surface, breathing air through a siphon. Each larva turns into a pupa (c), which also lives near the surface. When the adult insect has formed inside the pupa, the skin splits and the Gnat crawls out (d).

Butterflies

a Egg

b Larva (caterpillar)

c Pupa

d Adult Butterfly

The Meadow Brown Butterfly lays a single egg on grass (a). The caterpillar (b) comes out of the egg and spends the winter in this form. Early the next summer, it turns into a pupa (c).
Inside the pupa, or chrysalis, the body of the caterpillar breaks down and reforms into the body of the Butterfly. This takes about four weeks. Then the pupa splits, and the adult emerges. It rests while its crumpled wings spread out and dry. Then it is ready to fly (d).

Stag Beetles

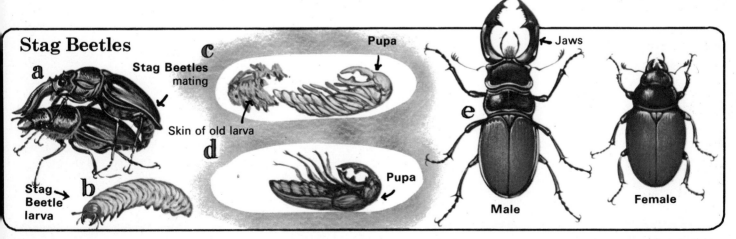

a

b Stag Beetle larva

c Stag Beetles mating

Skin of old larva

Pupa

d Pupa

e

Jaws

Male

Female

After mating (a), the female Stag Beetle lays her eggs in holes in rotten trees. The young larva (b) lives for three years burrowing through the soft wood of the tree.

Then, the larva stops feeding, makes a pupal cell in the wood and becomes a pupa (c). It lies on its back to protect the newly-formed limbs until they harden (d).

It emerges as an adult Beetle (e). The males have large jaws which look like a stag's antlers. They use them for fighting and to attract the female.

9

Insects in the Garden

A good place to start a study of insects is in your own garden. If you do not have a garden then look in your nearest park or open space. Make a chart of the insects you find there each month. In winter, look under stones, the bark of tree stumps and dead leaves. It is even worth looking in a garden shed. Some insects spend the winter without moving or feeding. This is called hibernation. If you find a hibernating insect, do not disturb it.

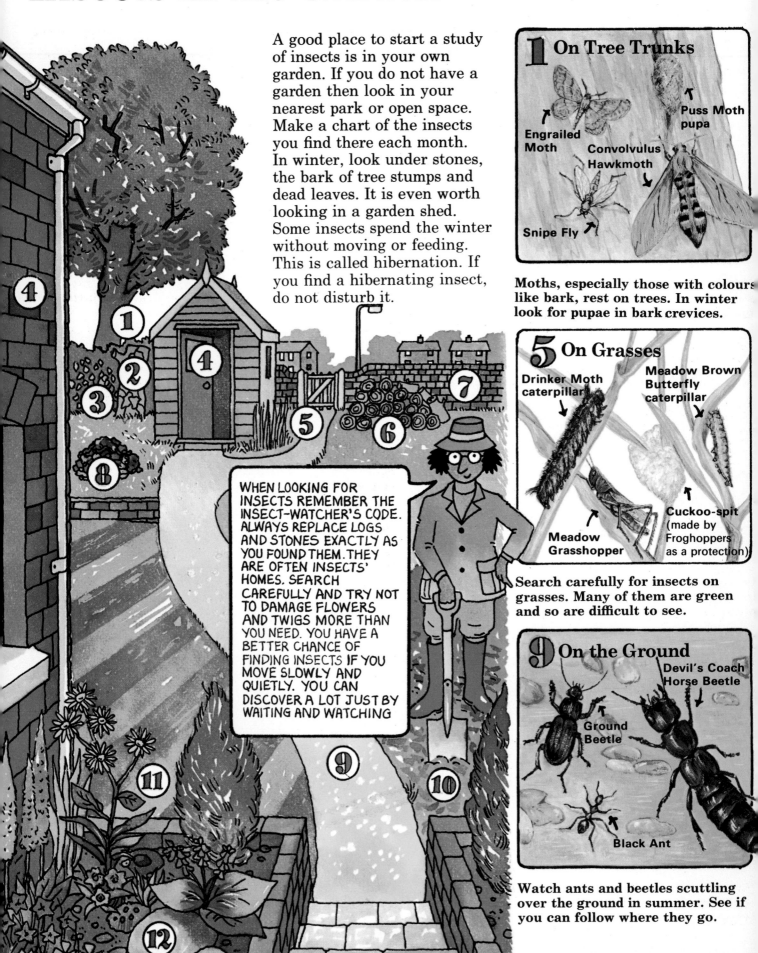

WHEN LOOKING FOR INSECTS REMEMBER THE INSECT-WATCHER'S CODE. ALWAYS REPLACE LOGS AND STONES EXACTLY AS YOU FOUND THEM. THEY ARE OFTEN INSECTS' HOMES. SEARCH CAREFULLY AND TRY NOT TO DAMAGE FLOWERS AND TWIGS MORE THAN YOU NEED. YOU HAVE A BETTER CHANCE OF FINDING INSECTS IF YOU MOVE SLOWLY AND QUIETLY. YOU CAN DISCOVER A LOT JUST BY WAITING AND WATCHING

1 On Tree Trunks

Engrailed Moth
Puss Moth pupa
Convolvulus Hawkmoth
Snipe Fly

Moths, especially those with colours like bark, rest on trees. In winter look for pupae in bark crevices.

5 On Grasses

Drinker Moth caterpillar
Meadow Brown Butterfly caterpillar
Meadow Grasshopper
Cuckoo-spit (made by Froghoppers as a protection)

Search carefully for insects on grasses. Many of them are green and so are difficult to see.

9 On the Ground

Devil's Coach Horse Beetle
Ground Beetle
Black Ant

Watch ants and beetles scuttling over the ground in summer. See if you can follow where they go.

2 Under Bark

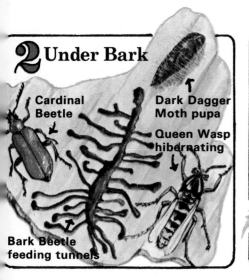

Cardinal Beetle

Dark Dagger Moth pupa

Queen Wasp hibernating

Bark Beetle feeding tunnels

Queen Wasps and Beetles sometimes hibernate under loose bark. Look for Bark Beetle tunnels.

3 On Leaves and Stems

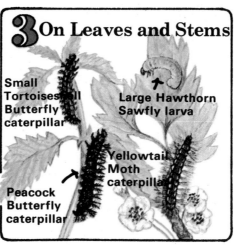

Small Tortoiseshell Butterfly caterpillar

Large Hawthorn Sawfly larva

Yellowtail Moth caterpillar

Peacock Butterfly caterpillar

Most caterpillars feed on leaves. Look for them in spring and summer, particularly on hedges.

4 House and Outhouse

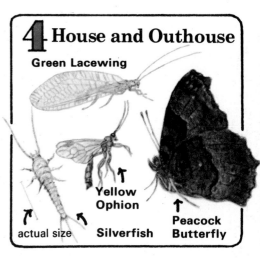

Green Lacewing

Yellow Ophion

actual size

Silverfish

Peacock Butterfly

If you search a shed in winter, you may find a Peacock Butterfly or a Lacewing.

6 In Woodpiles

Butterfly pupae

Herald Moth

Large Yellow Underwing Moth

In winter, these insects hibernate in sheltered places such as wood piles. Never disturb them there.

7 On Walls

Flower (or Potter) Bee

Small Copper Butterfly

Wall Brown Butterfly

Wall-Mason Wasp

These insects like to settle on walls, particularly if the walls face the sun.

8 In the Rubbish Heap

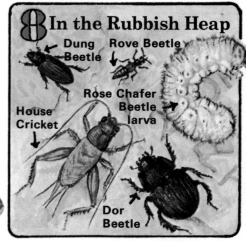

Dung Beetle

Rove Beetle

Rose Chafer Beetle larva

House Cricket

Dor Beetle

These insects feed on waste matter. You are most likely to find them in a rubbish heap.

10 In the Soil

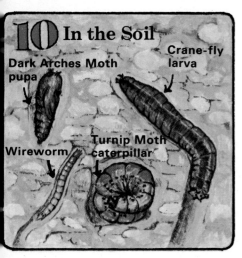

Dark Arches Moth pupa

Crane-fly larva

Turnip Moth caterpillar

Wireworm

You will have to dig in the ground to find these insects. The larvae (young insects) feed on roots.

11 On Flowers

Silver-Washed Fritillary

Hornet

In summer, look for insects like these feeding on the nectar and pollen of flowers.

12 Under Stones

Earwig protecting its eggs

Violet Ground Beetle

Garden Tiger Moth caterpillar

Lift up large stones to discover these insects. They like to live in dark, damp places.

Insects in a Tree

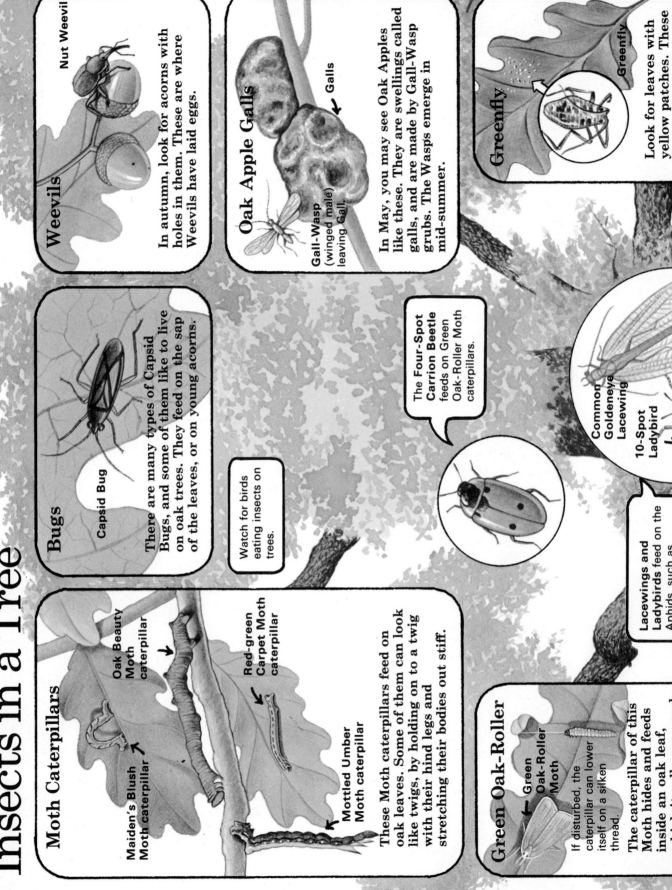

Weevils

Nut Weevil

In autumn, look for acorns with holes in them. These are where Weevils have laid eggs.

Oak Apple Galls

Galls

Gall-Wasp (winged male) leaving Gall.

In May, you may see Oak Apples like these. They are swellings called galls, and are made by Gall-Wasp grubs. The Wasps emerge in mid-summer.

Greenfly

Greenfly

Look for leaves with yellow patches. These are caused by Greenfly feeding.

Bugs

Capsid Bug

There are many types of Capsid Bugs, and some of them like to live on oak trees. They feed on the sap of the leaves, or on young acorns.

Watch for birds eating insects on trees.

The **Four-Spot Carrion Beetle** feeds on Green Oak-Roller Moth caterpillars.

Common Goldeneye Lacewing

10-Spot Ladybird

Lacewings and **Ladybirds** feed on the Aphids, such as Greenfly, that live on oak trees.

Moth Caterpillars

Maiden's Blush Moth caterpillar

Oak Beauty Moth caterpillar

Red-green Carpet Moth caterpillar

Mottled Umber Moth caterpillar

These Moth caterpillars feed on oak leaves. Some of them can look like twigs, by holding on to a twig with their hind legs and stretching their bodies out stiff.

Green Oak-Roller

Green Oak-Roller Moth

If disturbed, the caterpillar can lower itself on a silken thread.

The caterpillar of this Moth hides and feeds inside an oak leaf, which it rolls over and binds with silk.

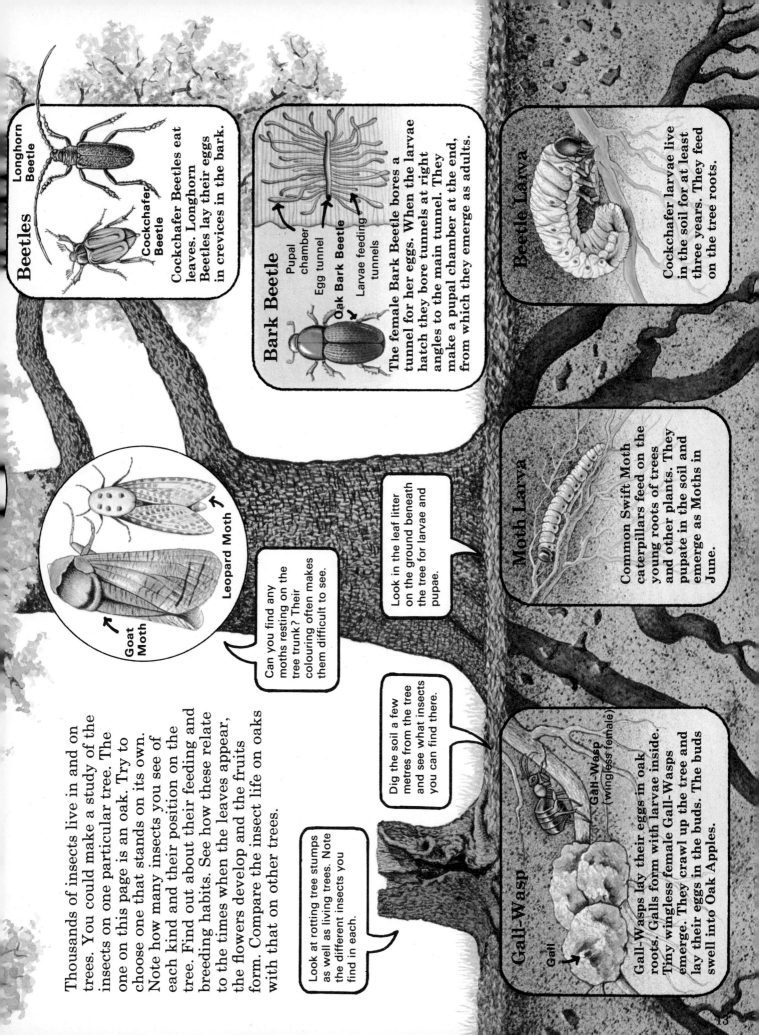

Thousands of insects live in and on trees. You could make a study of the insects on one particular tree. The one on this page is an oak. Try to choose one that stands on its own. Note how many insects you see of each kind and their position on the tree. Find out about their feeding and breeding habits. See how these relate to the times when the leaves appear, the flowers develop and the fruits form. Compare the insect life on oaks with that on other trees.

Beetles

Longhorn Beetle

Cockchafer Beetle

Cockchafer Beetles eat leaves. Longhorn Beetles lay their eggs in crevices in the bark.

Bark Beetle

Pupal chamber

Egg tunnel

Larvae feeding tunnels

Oak Bark Beetle

The female Bark Beetle bores a tunnel for her eggs. When the larvae hatch they bore tunnels at right angles to the main tunnel. They make a pupal chamber at the end, from which they emerge as adults.

Beetle Larva

Cockchafer larvae live in the soil for at least three years. They feed on the tree roots.

Goat Moth

Leopard Moth

Can you find any moths resting on the tree trunk? Their colouring often makes them difficult to see.

Look in the leaf litter on the ground beneath the tree for larvae and pupae.

Moth Larva

Common Swift Moth caterpillars feed on the young roots of trees and other plants. They pupate in the soil and emerge as Moths in June.

Look at rotting tree stumps as well as living trees. Note the different insects you find in each.

Dig the soil a few metres from the tree and see what insects you can find there.

Gall-Wasp

Gall

Gall-Wasp (wingless female)

Gall-Wasps lay their eggs in oak roots. Galls form with larvae inside. Tiny wingless female Gall-Wasps emerge. They crawl up the tree and lay their eggs in the buds. The buds swell into Oak Apples.

Pond Insects

The best time of year to find all these pond insects is in early summer. This is the time when the Dragonflies and other flying insects change from being nymphs, larvae and pupae living in the water. Look in different places around the pond. Watch the insects that fly over the pond and those that are on the surface. Search among the water weeds and dip with your net to find insects that live in the water.

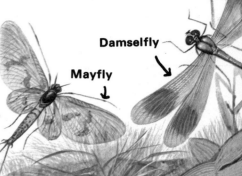

Damselfly

Mayfly

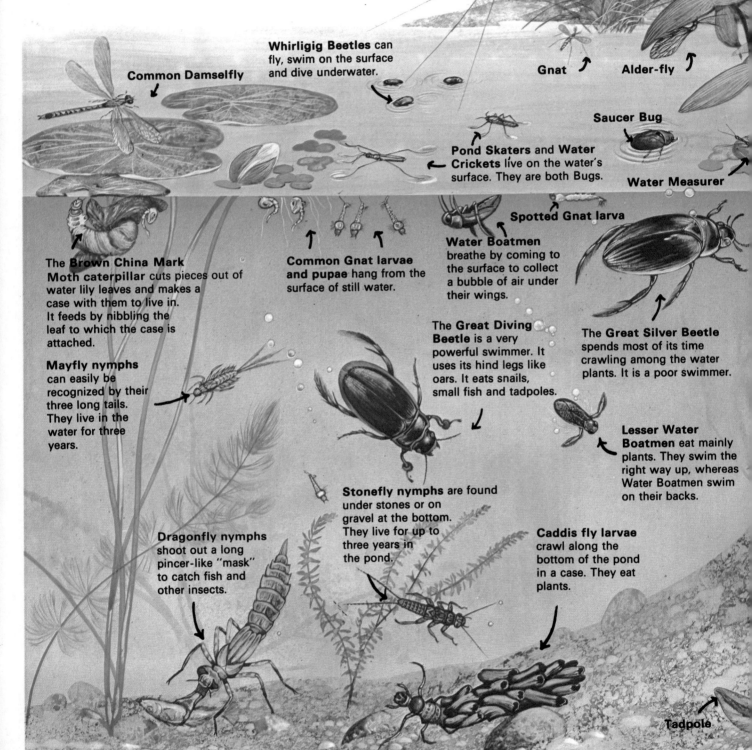

Common Damselfly

Whirligig Beetles can fly, swim on the surface and dive underwater.

Gnat

Alder-fly

Saucer Bug

Pond Skaters and **Water Crickets** live on the water's surface. They are both Bugs.

Water Measurer

Spotted Gnat larva

The Brown China Mark Moth caterpillar cuts pieces out of water lily leaves and makes a case with them to live in. It feeds by nibbling the leaf to which the case is attached.

Mayfly nymphs can easily be recognized by their three long tails. They live in the water for three years.

Common Gnat larvae and pupae hang from the surface of still water.

Water Boatmen breathe by coming to the surface to collect a bubble of air under their wings.

The Great Diving Beetle is a very powerful swimmer. It uses its hind legs like oars. It eats snails, small fish and tadpoles.

The Great Silver Beetle spends most of its time crawling among the water plants. It is a poor swimmer.

Lesser Water Boatmen eat mainly plants. They swim the right way up, whereas Water Boatmen swim on their backs.

Dragonfly nymphs shoot out a long pincer-like "mask" to catch fish and other insects.

Stonefly nymphs are found under stones or on gravel at the bottom. They live for up to three years in the pond.

Caddis fly larvae crawl along the bottom of the pond in a case. They eat plants.

Tadpole

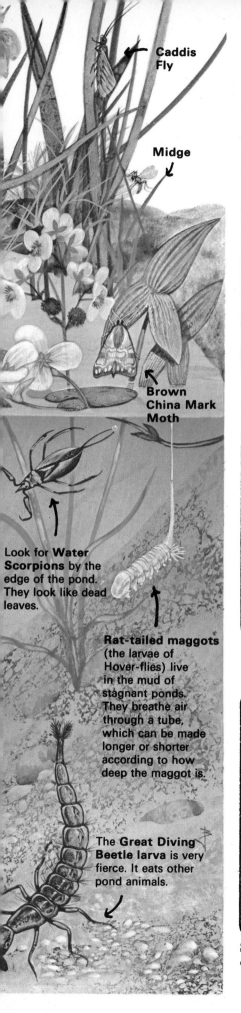

Caddis Fly

Midge

Brown China Mark Moth

Look for **Water Scorpions** by the edge of the pond. They look like dead leaves.

Rat-tailed maggots (the larvae of Hover-flies) live in the mud of stagnant ponds. They breathe air through a tube, which can be made longer or shorter according to how deep the maggot is.

The **Great Diving Beetle larva** is very fierce. It eats other pond animals.

TAKE A POND NET FOR CATCHING INSECTS THAT LIVE IN THE WATER OR ON THE SURFACE. YOU CAN USE A PLASTIC SIEVE IN SHALLOW WATER

What You Need

YOU ALSO NEED A SHALLOW WHITE DISH TO TIP YOUR CATCH INTO AND A TEASPOON FOR PUTTING IT INTO A SCREW-TOPPED CONTAINER. A TROWEL IS USEFUL FOR SCOOPING MUD BY THE POND'S EDGE

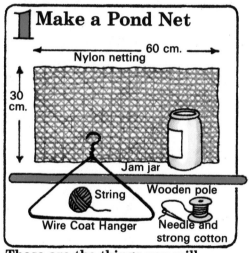

1 Make a Pond Net

60 cm.
Nylon netting
30 cm.
Jam jar
String
Wire Coat Hanger
Wooden pole
Needle and strong cotton

These are the things you will need for making a pond net.

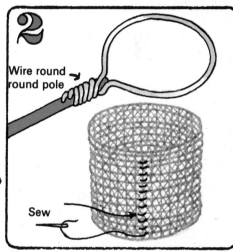

2

Wire round round pole

Sew

Bend the hanger into a hoop with pliers and wind the ends round the pole. Sew the edges of the netting.

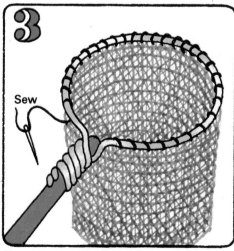

3

Sew

Sew the long edge of the netting over the wire frame.

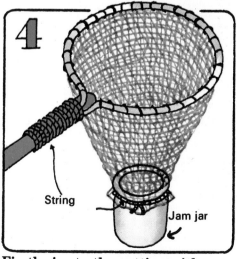

4

String

Jam jar

Fix the jar to the netting with string. Tie the string over the wire on the pole to strengthen it.

Insect Senses

Insects do not sense things in the same way that we do. They do not have a nose for smelling. However, insects can feel, smell and taste with their antennae. Some can also taste with their feet, while the hairs on an insect's body help it to feel.

Most insects have **hairs** on their bodies. These hairs are stiff and are connected to nerve cells. The insect can feel every movement of the hairs.

Simple eyes

The **antennae** are an insect's most important sense organs. They are sensitive to heat and damp, as well as being used for smelling and tasting. Only parts of the Bluebottle's antennae are shown. The main parts are in front of the head.

Insects have two kinds of **eyes**—simple eyes, called ocelli, and compound eyes. The compound eyes are made up of thousands of separate lenses.

Insects do not focus their eyes in the same way that we do. They can, however, detect even the slightest movement. Some insects can see forwards, backwards and downwards all at the same time.

Bluebottle (or Blow-fly)

Some insects, such as Butterflies, Bees and Blowflies, can taste with their **feet**. When they land on something sweet, they immediately put out their proboscis and start feeding.

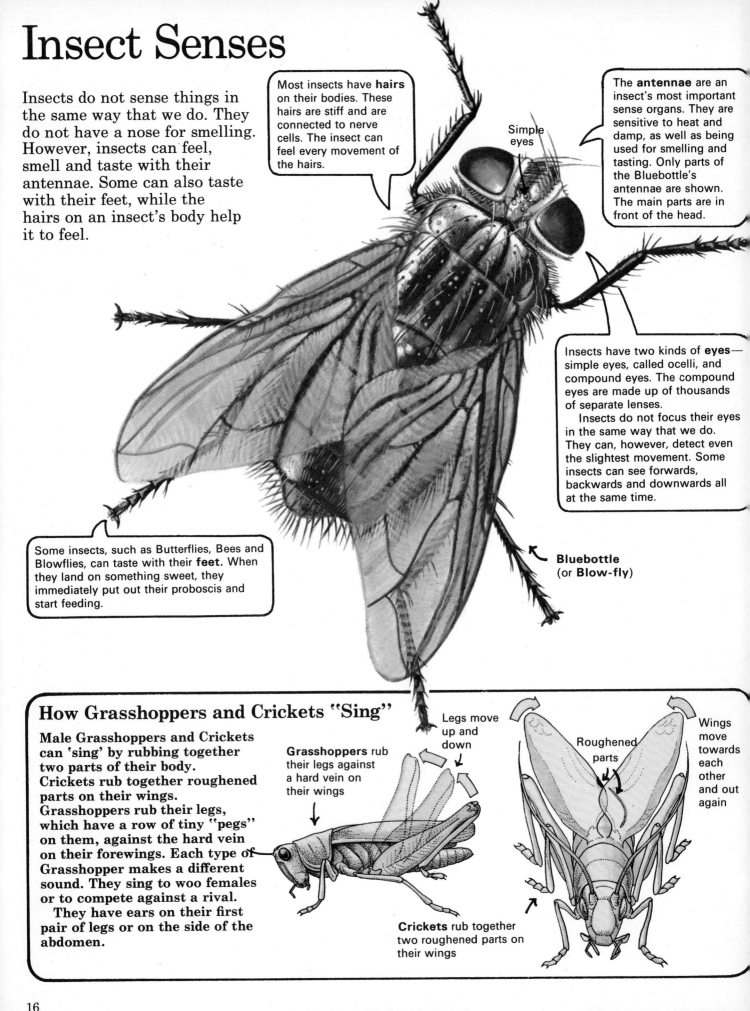

How Grasshoppers and Crickets "Sing"

Male Grasshoppers and Crickets can 'sing' by rubbing together two parts of their body. Crickets rub together roughened parts on their wings. Grasshoppers rub their legs, which have a row of tiny "pegs" on them, against the hard vein on their forewings. Each type of Grasshopper makes a different sound. They sing to woo females or to compete against a rival.

They have ears on their first pair of legs or on the side of the abdomen.

Legs move up and down

Grasshoppers rub their legs against a hard vein on their wings

Crickets rub together two roughened parts on their wings

Roughened parts

Wings move towards each other and out again

Antennae

Ants touching antennae

Emperor Moth

Ants smell with their antennae. When two Ants meet they touch antennae. Every Ants' nest has a different smell. If the Ants are not from the same nest they will fight one another, sometimes to the death.

The male Emperor Moth has feathered antennae. It uses them to find food and a mate. It can pick up the scent of a female from several miles away.

Longhorned Beetles tap trees with their antennae to find suitable places for laying eggs and to recognize one another in the dark.

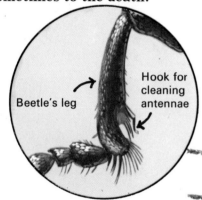

Beetle's leg

Hook for cleaning antennae

Cleaning hook

Longhorn Beetle's antenna

Most insects have some method of cleaning their antennae. Bees and some Beetles have a hair hook on their forelegs.

Hairs

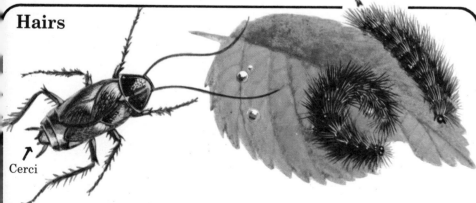

Cerci

Crickets and Cockroaches have tail feelers at the end of their abdomen. These are called cerci and are sensitive to touch.

The stiff hairs on a caterpillar respond to sound waves in the air. If you clap or whistle near a caterpillar, watch how it curls up or suddenly "freezes".

Things to Do

1

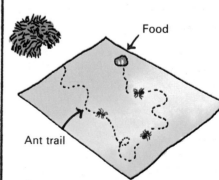

ANTS CAN LEAVE A SCENT TRAIL. THEY PRESS THEIR BODIES ON THE GROUND, LEAVING A SMELL FOR OTHERS TO FOLLOW. IF YOU FIND A TRAIL, RUB PART OF IT OUT. WATCH WHAT THE ANTS DO

2

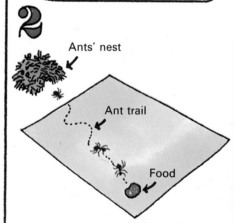

Ants' nest

Ant trail

Food

PUT A PIECE OF PAPER WITH FOOD ON IT NEAR AN ANTS' NEST. WATCH SEVERAL ANTS FIND THE FOOD. THEN MOVE THE FOOD TO ANOTHER PART OF THE PAPER.

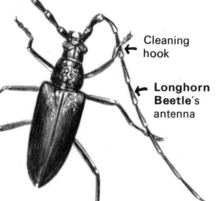

Food

Ant trail

WATCH WHAT THE ANTS COMING FROM THE NEST DO. DO THEY GO STRAIGHT TO THE FOOD? OR DO THEY GO FIRST TO WHERE THE FOOD WAS BEFORE YOU MOVED IT?

17

Watching Insects Move

Many insects have a particular way of moving. Once you can recognize their different movements you will be able to identify insects more easily. Insects that walk or run usually have long, thin legs. Insects that dig, such as Chafers or Dor Beetles, have forelegs that are shorter but stronger than the other two pairs. Insects that jump or swim often have specially developed hind-legs. Compare the way different insects fly. Wasps, Flies and Bees flap their wings faster than Butterflies.

Jumping

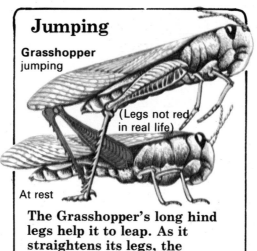

Grasshopper jumping

(Legs not red in real life)

At rest

The Grasshopper's long hind legs help it to leap. As it straightens its legs, the Grasshopper pushes itself high into the air.

Swimming

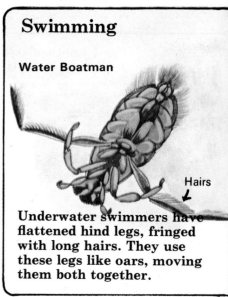

Water Boatman

Hairs

Underwater swimmers have flattened hind legs, fringed with long hairs. They use these legs like oars, moving them both together.

Walking on Water

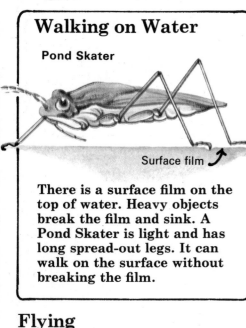

Pond Skater

Surface film

There is a surface film on the top of water. Heavy objects break the film and sink. A Pond Skater is light and has long spread-out legs. It can walk on the surface without breaking the film.

Digging

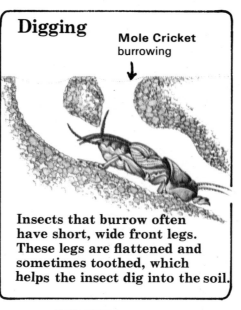

Mole Cricket burrowing

Insects that burrow often have short, wide front legs. These legs are flattened and sometimes toothed, which helps the insect dig into the soil.

How Caterpillars Move

1
2
3
4
5
6

Caterpillars have three pairs of walking legs and up to five pairs of false legs. They move each pair of false legs in turn.

Flying

Look at the different shapes of insects' wings, and watch how fast or slowly they fly. Look to see if they have one pair of wings or two.

When a **Beetle** flies it holds up its stiff wing-cases, to let its wings move easily. When it lands it folds its wings back under the wing-cases.

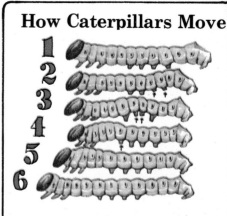

Wing-case

Halteres

Many **Butterflies** have square-shaped wings, that flap quite slowly.

Cockchafer Beetle

Flies have only one pair of wings. Instead of hind wings they have two knobs, called halteres. These help the insect to balance.

Walking on Land

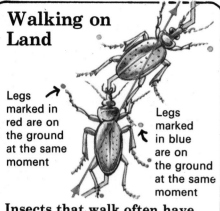

Legs marked in red are on the ground at the same moment

Legs marked in blue are on the ground at the same moment

Insects that walk often have long thin legs, which are all alike. They walk by moving three legs at a time and balancing on the other three.

Looper Caterpillars

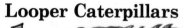

1

Front legs   Hind legs

2

3

4

A "looper" caterpillar moves forward by bringing forward its hind legs (1, 2) and then stretching out its front legs (3, 4).

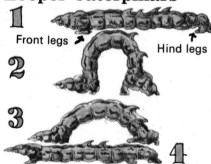

Hawkmoths have pointed wings. They can fly fast and for a long time. In flight the two pairs of wings are joined and flap as one.

Catch on wing holds wings together

Hooks

Bees and Wasps have two pairs of wings. They are held together during flight by a tiny row of hooks.

How Flies Walk Upside Down

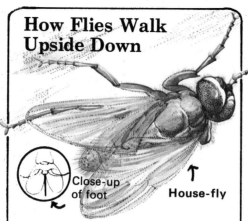

Close-up of foot

House-fly

House-flies have sticky, hairy pads on their feet. Because the fly is so light, the grip of the pads is strong enough to hold it on almost any surface.

How Click Beetles Click

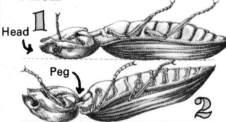

Head   1

Peg   2

If a Click Beetle falls on its back (1), it arches its body until only its head and tail touch the ground. A peg on its thorax makes it double up (2). Its wing-cases hit the ground and the beetle is thrown into the air, with a "clicking" sound.

How Springtails Jump

1 At rest

2 Jumping

Fork

3 Landing

The Springtail cannot fly, but it can jump. It has a forked tail which folds under its body. If the Springtail is disturbed, the tail flicks down on the ground and throws the insect forward.

FIND OUT WHAT HAPPENS WHEN DIFFERENT INSECTS MEET WATER, OTHER INSECTS OR THINGS IN THEIR WAY. PUT DOWN TWIGS, STONES OR SOME PAPER. NOTE DOWN WHAT YOU SEE

SEE WHETHER INSECTS MOVE AT THE SAME SPEED ON DIFFERENT KINDS OF SURFACE. COMPARE HOW THEY MOVE ON SOIL, GRASS AND WOOD

SMOKE A PLATE OVER A CANDLE. PUT THE PLATE ON THE GROUND AND WATCH INSECTS MOVE OVER IT. LOOK AT THE DIFFERENT TRACKS WITH A POCKET LENS AND SEE WHAT PATTERNS EACH INSECT MAKES

Watching Insects Feed

Insects feed on almost every kind of animal and plant. Some of them, such as Cockroaches, will eat almost anything, but most insects feed on one particular kind of food. There are insects that feed on cork, paper, clothes, ink, cigarettes, carpets, flour—even film or shoe-polish!

The diet of an insect may change at different stages in its life. Some insects eat only animals when they are larvae and plants when they are adult or vice versa. But most insects eat either plants or animals.

Insects that eat plants are called herbivores. More than half of all insects eat plants. Some feed on the leaves, flowers or seeds of plants, others bite the roots or suck the sap from inside plant stems. Some insects feed on nectar and pollen. You can find out more about them on pages 22–3.

Some insects feed on animals smaller than themselves, or suck the blood from larger ones, sometimes after paralyzing or killing them. Female Mosquitoes and Horseflies usually need to have a meal of mammal's boold before they can produce eggs. Many insects feed inside the bodies of other animals, and live there all the time. They are called parasites.

Some insects are called scavengers. They eat any decaying material that they find in the soil, such as animals that are already dead. They also feed on the dung of animals. Flea larvae eat the droppings of adult Fleas, as well as dirt and skin fragments.

Plant Feeders

1 Leaf-Eaters

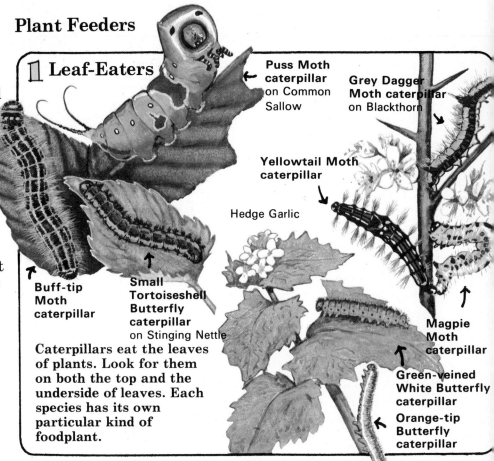

Puss Moth caterpillar on Common Sallow

Grey Dagger Moth caterpillar on Blackthorn

Yellowtail Moth caterpillar

Hedge Garlic

Buff-tip Moth caterpillar

Small Tortoiseshell Butterfly caterpillar on Stinging Nettle

Magpie Moth caterpillar

Green-veined White Butterfly caterpillar

Orange-tip Butterfly caterpillar

Caterpillars eat the leaves of plants. Look for them on both the top and the underside of leaves. Each species has its own particular kind of foodplant.

2 Wood-borers

Wood Wasps lay their eggs in pine trees. The larvae eat the soft wood. **Giant Wood Wasp**

3 Sap-Feeders

Bugs, such as Greenfly and Blackfly pierce leaves and plant stems and suck the sap inside.

Piercing tube

Greenfly

4 Leaf Miners

Blotch mine—caterpillars eat around themselves

Serpentine mine—caterpillars move forward as they eat

Caterpillars of tiny Moths and Flies tunnel between the two surfaces of a leaf and eat the tissues inside.

5 Seed-Eaters

Nut Weevil

Larva inside nut

The female Nut Weevil bores a hole in newly formed hazel nuts and acorns and lays an egg. The grub hatches and feeds on the nut. The nut falls to the ground and the larva eats its way out and pupates in the soil.

Insects' Mouthparts

Insects either bite and chew solid food, or they suck liquids. Insects that suck have a hollow tube, called a proboscis. Bees, Butterflies and Moths suck nectar from inside flowers. Bugs can pierce plant stems and suck the sap inside. Mosquitoes pierce the skin of animals or humans and suck their blood. Insects that bite and chew have three pairs of jaws—a large pair called mandibles, a smaller pair called maxillae and a third pair which are joined together to form a kind of lower lip.

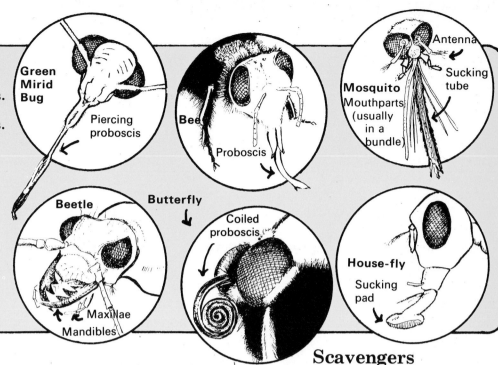

Green Mirid Bug — Piercing proboscis

Bee — Proboscis

Mosquito Mouthparts (usually in a bundle) — Antenna — Sucking tube

Beetle — Maxillae — Mandibles

Butterfly — Coiled proboscis

House-fly — Sucking pad

Animal Feeders

1 Aphid Eaters

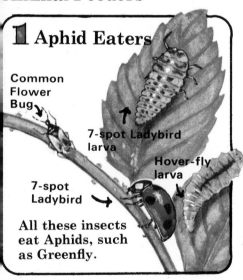

Common Flower Bug

7-spot Ladybird larva

Hover-fly larva

7-spot Ladybird

All these insects eat Aphids, such as Greenfly.

3 Wasps

Wasps sting caterpillars and take them to their nest to feed their larvae.

Red-Banded Sand Wasp

5 Dragonflies

Some Dragonflies are often called "Hawkers" because they fly so fast and overpower other insects.

2 Tiger Beetles

Tiger Beetles run fast and catch other insects with their strong mandibles. Their larva burrows a hole in the sand and waits for its prey.

Larva in burrow →

4 Mosquitoes

Mosquitoes usually fly by night. The female sucks blood; the male sucks nectar from flowers.

Skin

6 Robber-flies

Robber-flies pounce on insects in the air and suck them dry.

Scavengers

1 Blow-flies

Blow-flies lay their eggs on meat. The maggots eat the meat when they hatch.

Bluebottle (Blow-fly)

Meat

2 Dor Beetles

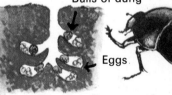

Balls of dung

Eggs

Dor Beetles dig tunnels under cow dung. The female lays her eggs in chambers. The larvae feed on balls of dung.

3 Burying Beetles

Burying Beetles dig a hole and pull dead animals underground. They lay their eggs near the corpse.

21

Insects and Flowers

Insects visit flowers for food. Moths and Butterflies feed on the nectar, a sweet liquid found inside most flowers. Honey Bees collect pollen, the yellow dust inside flowers, as well as nectar, for feeding their larvae.

Flowers do not need the nectar they produce, except to attract insects. The insects help the flowers to make new seeds. Most insects that visit flowers are hairy. When they feed on a flower they become dusted with pollen from the ripe stamens (the male parts inside a flower). Then they visit other flowers of the same species, and some of the sticky pollen may be accidentally brushed off onto the stigmas (the female parts of the flower).

This is called pollination. Only when a flower has been pollinated can new seeds start growing.

Flowers that attract insects usually have a strong scent. Insects do not see colours as we do. Flowers that look one colour to us, such as the yellow Tormentil, appear white with dark centres to an insect.

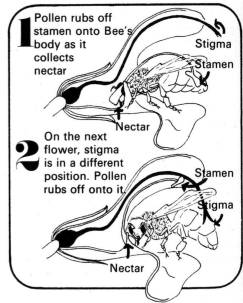

1 Pollen rubs off stamen onto Bee's body as it collects nectar

Stigma

Stamen

Nectar

2 On the next flower, stigma is in a different position. Pollen rubs off onto it.

Stamen

Stigma

Nectar

Wasps, like Bees, collect nectar. This they eat themselves or store for their young. But, unlike Bees, they do not collect and store pollen.

Watch how a Butterfly extends its long proboscis into a flower as soon as it lands. Butterflies feed from bright-coloured flowers that have a strong scent. Most flowers that Butterflies like are red, orange or pink. These are colours that Butterflies can see well.

Nectar Guides

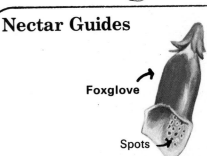

Foxglove

Spots

Some flowers that insects visit have lines or spots on their petals, pointing to where the nectar is. These patterns are called nectar guides. Flowers that have nectar guides are usually those where nectar is deeply hidden.

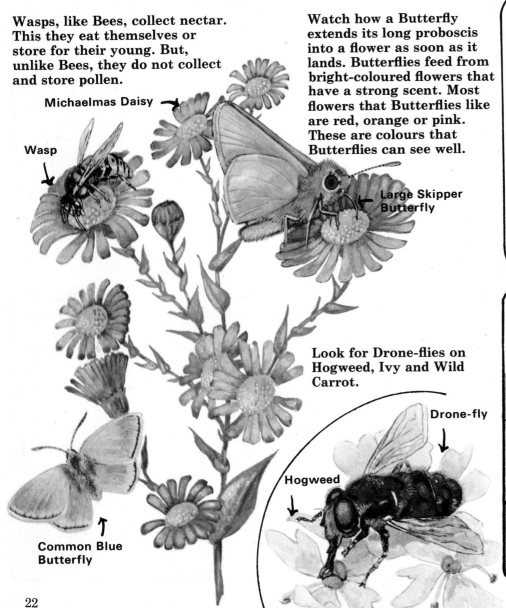

Michaelmas Daisy

Wasp

Large Skipper Butterfly

Look for Drone-flies on Hogweed, Ivy and Wild Carrot.

Drone-fly

Hogweed

Common Blue Butterfly

Make a Butterfly Garden

Try growing some of these plants to attract Butterflies. They feed on flowers like Buddleia and some of them lay eggs on weeds such as Ragwort, Nettles and Thistles.

THISTLE

BUDDLEIA

GOLDEN

1 Feeding on Flowers

Garden Chafer Beetle

Beetles have mouthparts that bite and chew. They cannot suck nectar like Bees, so they can only feed on flowers where the nectar is easy to get at.

2

Hover-fly

Proboscis

Some Flies that suck nectar look like Bees. They have hairy bodies and their tongues are longer than those of other Flies. Look for them on wide-open flowers.

3

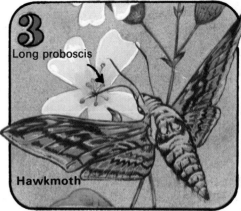

Long proboscis

Hawkmoth

Most Moths fly at dusk or at night. They are attracted to pale-coloured flowers that can be seen easily in the dark. The nectar is stored deep inside the flower.

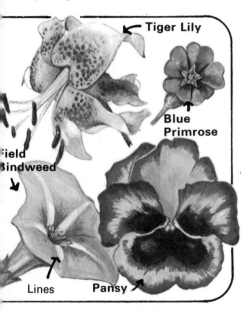

Tiger Lily

Blue Primrose

Field Bindweed

Lines

Pansy

4

Bumble Bee

Proboscis

Bees only gather nectar from one species of flower at a time. Watch this for yourself. Follow a single Bee and see what kind of flowers it visits.

5

Pollen on legs

Honey Bee

Honey Bees collect nectar and pollen. Nectar is sucked up through the tongue. Pollen is packed on the hind legs and held there by stiff bristles.

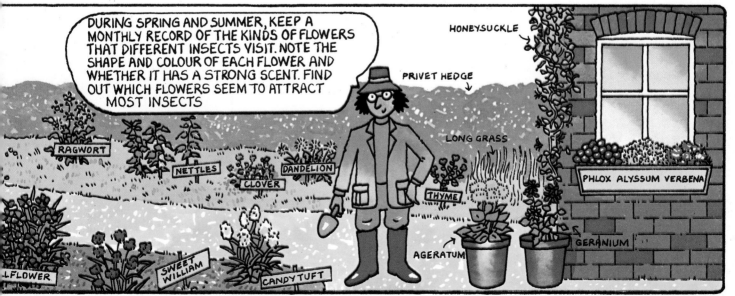

DURING SPRING AND SUMMER, KEEP A MONTHLY RECORD OF THE KINDS OF FLOWERS THAT DIFFERENT INSECTS VISIT. NOTE THE SHAPE AND COLOUR OF EACH FLOWER AND WHETHER IT HAS A STRONG SCENT. FIND OUT WHICH FLOWERS SEEM TO ATTRACT MOST INSECTS

HONEYSUCKLE

PRIVET HEDGE

LONG GRASS

PHLOX ALYSSUM VERBENA

RAGWORT

NETTLES

DANDELION

CLOVER

THYME

AGERATUM

GERANIUM

LFLOWER

SWEET WILLIAM

CANDYTUFT

Ants and Bees

Ants and Bees are "social insects." This means that they live in colonies, which may consist of thousands of insects, and share their food and work.

In any colony there are three kinds of insect: a queen, who is the only egg-laying female, males, called drones, whose only job is to mate with the queen, and undeveloped females, called workers, who do all the work in the colony. Each worker has a particular task; either to collect food, to care for the eggs and larvae or to repair or guard the nest.

An Ants' Nest

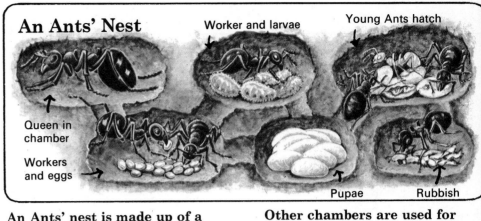

Worker and larvae

Young Ants hatch

Queen in chamber

Workers and eggs

Pupae

Rubbish

An Ants' nest is made up of a network of chambers and passages. The queen has a chamber of her own and there are separate chambers for eggs, larvae and pupae.

Other chambers are used for storing food or for rubbish. The Ants can change the temperature of the nest by opening or closing some of the passages.

1 How Ants are Born

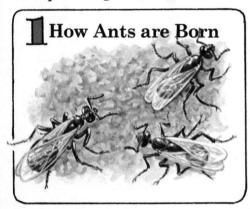

In summer, when the weather is warm, the winged males and the queen Ants leave the nest on a mating flight. After mating the males die. The queens fly to the ground.

2

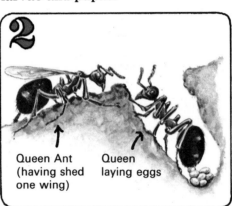

Queen Ant (having shed one wing)

Queen laying eggs

Each queen starts a new nest. She rubs or bites off her wings. Then she finds, or makes, a space in the soil where she can lay her first batch of eggs.

3

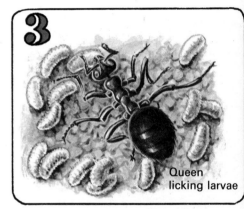

Queen licking larvae

When the larvae hatch, the queen feeds them with her own saliva. Later they emerge as worker Ants. They take over the job of looking after the nest and the eggs.

4

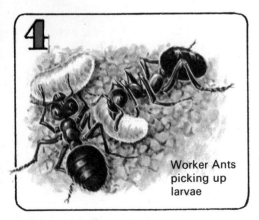

Worker Ants picking up larvae

Now the queen does nothing but lay more eggs. Workers feed the larvae and lick them clean. They even cut the pupae open to let the new Ants climb out.

Food

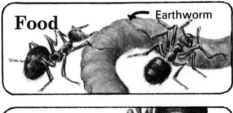

Earthworm

Aphid

Some Ants go out collecting small insects, worms and other food. Others lick the sweet honeydew that Aphids on nearby plants produce.

Defence

Jaws

Cleaning

Worker moving rubbish

Some Ants guard the nest. They wait by the entrance, their jaws open. Ants keep their nest very clean. They remove rubbish to special chambers or take it outside.

Honey Bees

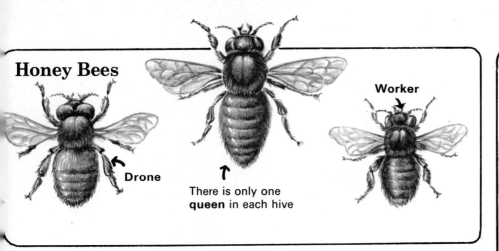

Worker

Drone

There is only one **queen** in each hive

These are three different kinds of Honey Bee that you will find in a hive. The only ones you will see flying around are the workers; the others stay in the hive.

The workers do all the jobs.

Young workers clean out cells, then, as they get older, they feed the larvae, build new cells and make honey. Later they collect nectar and pollen.

The Honeycomb

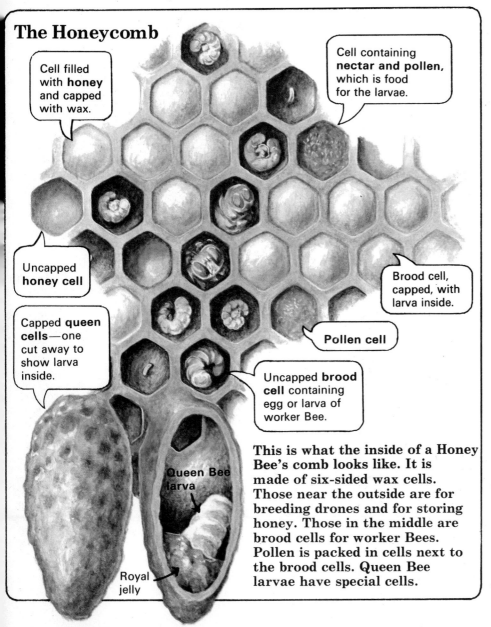

Cell filled with **honey** and capped with wax.

Cell containing **nectar and pollen**, which is food for the larvae.

Uncapped **honey cell**

Capped **queen cells**—one cut away to show larva inside.

Brood cell, capped, with larva inside.

Pollen cell

Uncapped **brood cell** containing egg or larva of worker Bee.

Queen Bee larva

Royal jelly

This is what the inside of a Honey Bee's comb looks like. It is made of six-sided wax cells. Those near the outside are for breeding drones and for storing honey. Those in the middle are brood cells for worker Bees. Pollen is packed in cells next to the brood cells. Queen Bee larvae have special cells.

How a Bee Grows

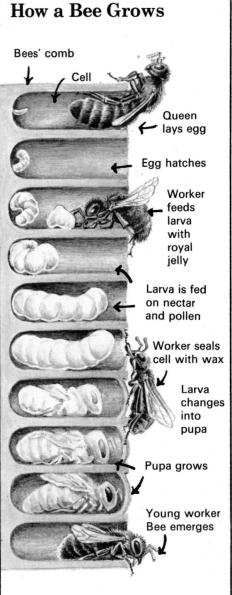

Bees' comb

Cell

Queen lays egg

Egg hatches

Worker feeds larva with royal jelly

Larva is fed on nectar and pollen

Worker seals cell with wax

Larva changes into pupa

Pupa grows

Young worker Bee emerges

The queen lays one egg in each cell. After three days the eggs hatch. At first, worker Bees feed the larvae with a special food called royal jelly. A few days later they are fed on nectar and pollen.

After six days the larvae are large and fat and fill their cells. Workers seal the cells with wax. Inside the cells the larvae pupate.

Two weeks later the young Bees bite through the wax and come out fully grown.

Collecting and Keeping Insects

If you want to collect insects you must keep them in surroundings that are as near as possible like their natural homes. When you find an insect, put it in a small tin with a sample of the plant on which you found it. This will help you to identify it. Number each tin. Put down the numbers in your notebook and, against each one, write a description of the insect and where you found it. Was it in a dry or damp place, a sunny or a shady place?

When you get home, make a suitable home for your insects. You will need containers that are big enough to hold enough food and give the insects some room to move around. It is best to use glass or clear plastic containers, then you can see what is happening inside.

It is usually a good idea to put some sand or soil at the bottom, with a stone and some plants. Keep the containers in a cool place away from the sunlight, but not in a draught.

Make sure you have a good supply of fresh food and change it each day. Most caterpillars have their own particular food plant and will not eat anything else. There is no point in collecting them unless you can give them the right food supply.

Look at the insects in your "zoo" every day and record any changes that you see. You could keep a note of how much caterpillars eat and measure their length, or what happens to them when they pupate.

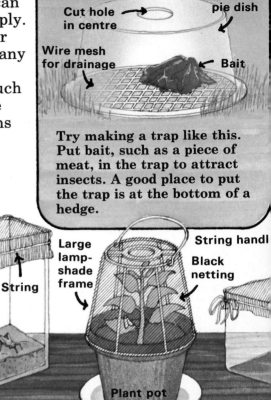

1 Collecting Crawling Insects

Cut hole in centre

Tin foil pie dish

Wire mesh for drainage

Bait

Try making a trap like this. Put bait, such as a piece of meat, in the trap to attract insects. A good place to put the trap is at the bottom of a hedge.

Muslin cover

String

Glass or plastic case

Soil

Large lamp-shade frame

String handle

Black netting

Plant pot

Saucer with water

Grasshopper and Cricket

In late summer, you may find Grasshoppers and Crickets. Keep them in a large glass case or jar and put sand in the bottom. Put in fresh grass every other day.

Moths

Make a Moth cage and keep it out of the sun. In hot weather, spray it with water. If you want the Moths to breed, put in the right plant for the larvae to feed on.

IT IS EASY TO COLLECT INSECTS BUT REMEMBER THAT THEY ARE VERY FRAGILE. HANDLE THEM AS LITTLE AS POSSIBLE AND DO NOT COLLECT MORE THAN YOU NEED TO STUDY. ONCE YOU HAVE FINISHED LOOKING AT THEM, TAKE THE INSECTS BACK TO THE PLACE WHERE YOU FOUND THEM. LET FLYING INSECTS GO AT DUSK SO THAT BIRDS OR CATS DO NOT ATTACK THEM

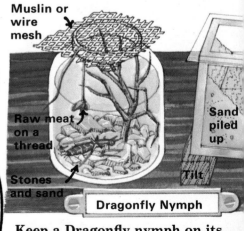

Muslin or wire mesh

Raw meat on a thread

Sand piled up

Stones and sand

Tilt

Dragonfly Nymph

Keep a Dragonfly nymph on its own in a large jam jar and feed it on raw meat. Put in an upright stick for the nymph to cling to when it sheds its skin.

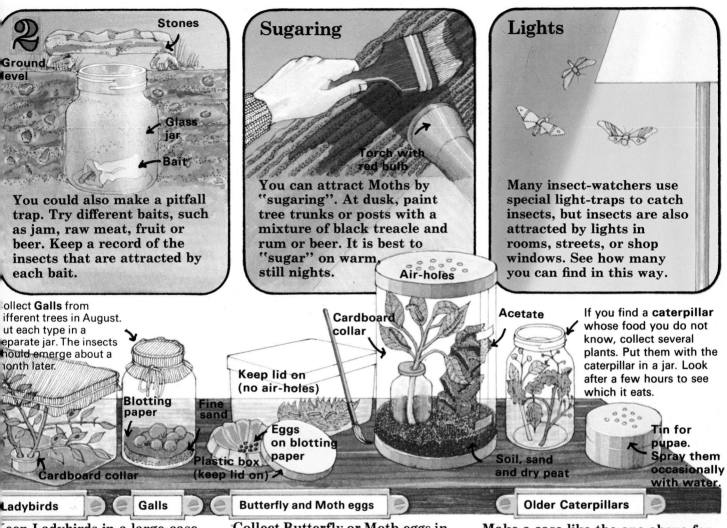

Sugaring

You can attract Moths by "sugaring". At dusk, paint tree trunks or posts with a mixture of black treacle and rum or beer. It is best to "sugar" on warm, still nights.

Lights

Many insect-watchers use special light-traps to catch insects, but insects are also attracted by lights in rooms, streets, or shop windows. See how many you can find in this way.

Stones

Ground level

Glass jar

Bait

You could also make a pitfall trap. Try different baits, such as jam, raw meat, fruit or beer. Keep a record of the insects that are attracted by each bait.

Torch with red bulb

Collect **Galls** from different trees in August. Put each type in a separate jar. The insects should emerge about a month later.

Air-holes

Cardboard collar

Keep lid on (no air-holes)

Blotting paper

Fine sand

Eggs on blotting paper

Plastic box (keep lid on)

Cardboard collar

Acetate

Soil, sand and dry peat

If you find a **caterpillar** whose food you do not know, collect several plants. Put them with the caterpillar in a jar. Look after a few hours to see which it eats.

Tin for pupae. Spray them occasionally with water.

Ladybirds	Galls	Butterfly and Moth eggs	Older Caterpillars

Keep Ladybirds in a large case like this to give them room to fly. They feed on Greenfly, which are often found on rose shoots. Cut off the whole shoot and keep it in water.

Collect Butterfly or Moth eggs in small boxes, and wait for them to hatch. When the caterpillars are a few hours old, transfer them with a brush to a box with a young leaf of their food plant. Put them on a new leaf each day.

Make a case like the one above for older caterpillars. Roll up a length of acetate and fix it with sticky tape. Put one half of a small tin on one end of the roll, and its lid on the other end.

Dig up pupae in the soil when they are hard and keep them in a tin. Caterpillars you already have will pupate on either the food plant, or the lid of the case, or the soil. In spring, when the pupae are ready to emerge, put them in a Moth cage like the one on the opposite page, on some damp moss. Put in a few twigs so that the

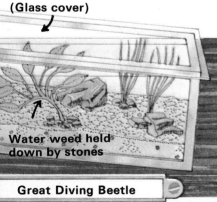

(Glass cover)

Water weed held down by stones

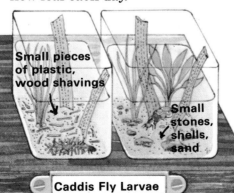

Small pieces of plastic, wood shavings

Small stones, shells, sand

Great Diving Beetle	Caddis Fly Larvae	

Great Diving Beetles and Water Boatmen are very fierce, so keep each one on its own. Feed them on maggots or raw meat attached to a thread, and changed daily.

See how Caddis Fly larvae make their protective cases. Collect several and carefully remove the larvae from their cases by prodding them with the blunt end

of a pin. Put them in separate aquariums with different materials in each, and watch what happens. Feed them on water weed.

Common Insects to Spot

Butterflies

Red Admiral. May to June and July to September.

Speckled Wood. April to June and August to September.

Orange-tip. May to June.

Small White. May to June and July to August.

Large White. May to August.

Green-veined White. May to June and August to September.

Underside of wing

Common Blue. May to June and August to September.

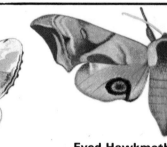

Wall. May to June and August to September.

Meadow Brown. Mid-June to September.

Moths

Eyed Hawkmoth. May to July.

Male Puss Moth. May to June.

Buff-tip. July to August.

Small Magpie. May to mid-July.

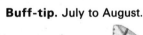

Brimstone. May to June and August to September.

Angle Shades. May to October.

Magpie. July to mid-August.

Vapourer. Late August to October.

Blood-vein. May to September.

Silver-Y. Migratory (June to October).

Burnished Brass. June to September.

Herald. Early Spring to Autumn.

Each caption tells you the time of year when you are most likely to see the insect. The Butterflies and Moths are drawn life size. The Beetles and Dragonflies are not.

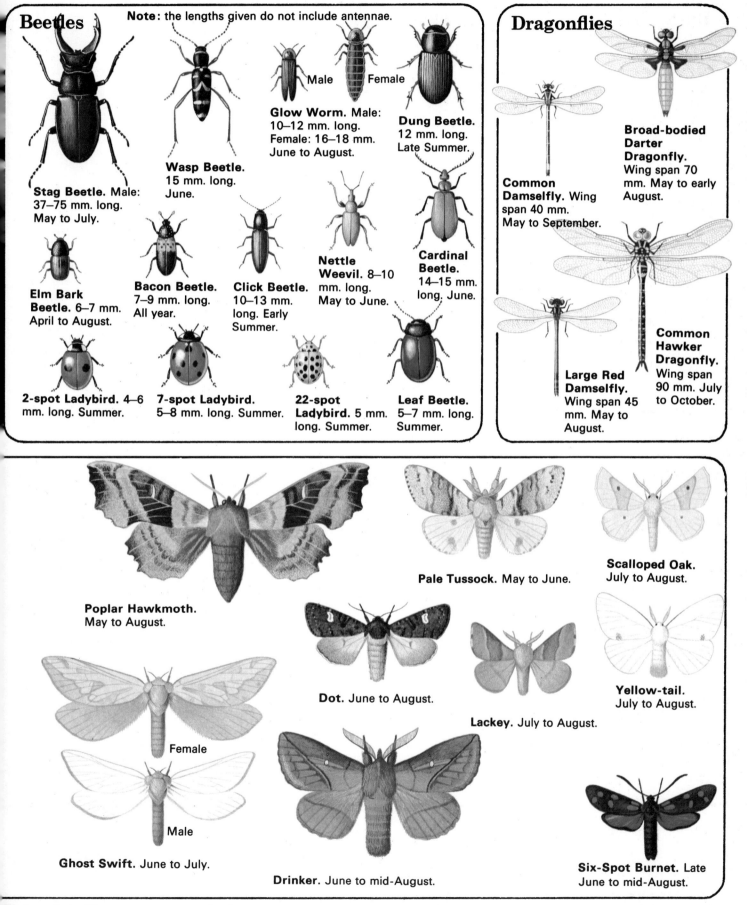

Beetles

Note: the lengths given do not include antennae.

Stag Beetle. Male: 37–75 mm. long. May to July.

Wasp Beetle. 15 mm. long. June.

Glow Worm. Male: 10–12 mm. long. Female: 16–18 mm. June to August.

Male   Female

Dung Beetle. 12 mm. long. Late Summer.

Elm Bark Beetle. 6–7 mm. April to August.

Bacon Beetle. 7–9 mm. long. All year.

Click Beetle. 10–13 mm. long. Early Summer.

Nettle Weevil. 8–10 mm. long. May to June.

Cardinal Beetle. 14–15 mm. long. June.

2-spot Ladybird. 4–6 mm. long. Summer.

7-spot Ladybird. 5–8 mm. long. Summer.

22-spot Ladybird. 5 mm. long. Summer.

Leaf Beetle. 5–7 mm. long. Summer.

Dragonflies

Common Damselfly. Wing span 40 mm. May to September.

Broad-bodied Darter Dragonfly. Wing span 70 mm. May to early August.

Large Red Damselfly. Wing span 45 mm. May to August.

Common Hawker Dragonfly. Wing span 90 mm. July to October.

Poplar Hawkmoth. May to August.

Pale Tussock. May to June.

Scalloped Oak. July to August.

Dot. June to August.

Lackey. July to August.

Yellow-tail. July to August.

Female

Male

Ghost Swift. June to July.

Drinker. June to mid-August.

Six-Spot Burnet. Late June to mid-August.

Remember, if you cannot see the insect you want to identify on these pages, turn to the page earlier in the book which deals with the kind of place where you found the insect.

Each caption tells you at what time of year you are most likely to see the insect. The lengths given do not include antennae.

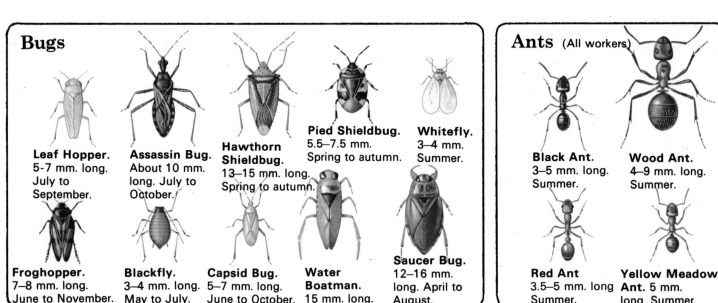

Bugs

Leaf Hopper. 5-7 mm. long. July to September.

Assassin Bug. About 10 mm. long. July to October.

Hawthorn Shieldbug. 13–15 mm. long. Spring to autumn.

Pied Shieldbug. 5.5–7.5 mm. Spring to autumn.

Whitefly. 3–4 mm. Summer.

Froghopper. 7–8 mm. long. June to November.

Blackfly. 3–4 mm. long. May to July.

Capsid Bug. 5–7 mm. long. June to October.

Water Boatman. 15 mm. long.

Saucer Bug. 12–16 mm. long. April to August.

Ants (All workers)

Black Ant. 3–5 mm. long. Summer.

Wood Ant. 4–9 mm. long. Summer.

Red Ant. 3.5–5 mm. long. Summer.

Yellow Meadow Ant. 5 mm. long. Summer.

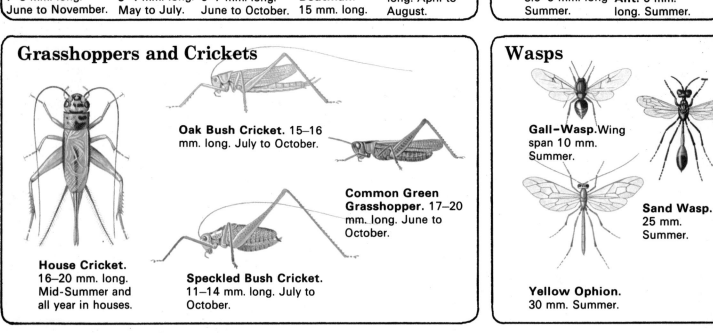

Grasshoppers and Crickets

Oak Bush Cricket. 15–16 mm. long. July to October.

Common Green Grasshopper. 17–20 mm. long. June to October.

House Cricket. 16–20 mm. long. Mid-Summer and all year in houses.

Speckled Bush Cricket. 11–14 mm. long. July to October.

Wasps

Gall-Wasp. Wing span 10 mm. Summer.

Sand Wasp. 25 mm. Summer.

Yellow Ophion. 30 mm. Summer.

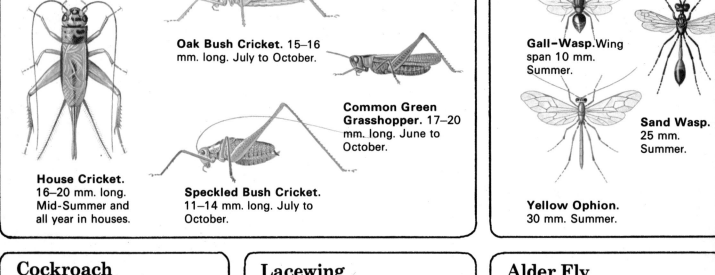

Cockroach

Common Cockroach. 24 mm. long. All year round in houses.

Lacewing

Green Lacewing. Wing span 30 mm. Summer.

Alder Fly

Alder Fly. Wing span 30 mm. May to June.

Earwig

Common Earwig. About 16 mm. long. All year, especially summer.

Scorpion Fly

Common Scorpion Fly. Wing span 30 mm. May to July.

Snake Fly

Snake Fly. Wing span 28 mm. May to July.

emember, if you cannot see the insect you want to identify on these pages, turn to the page earlier the book which deals with the kind of place where you found the insect.

Flies

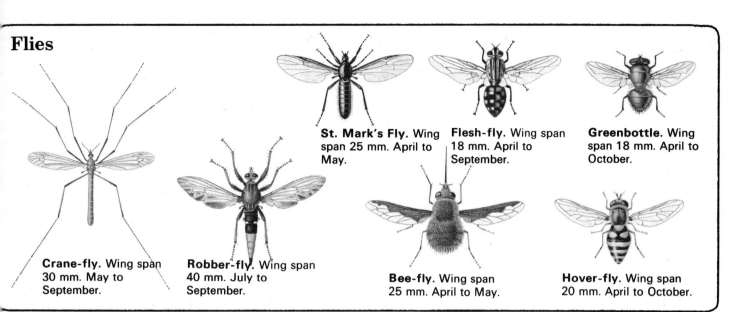

St. Mark's Fly. Wing span 25 mm. April to May.

Flesh-fly. Wing span 18 mm. April to September.

Greenbottle. Wing span 18 mm. April to October.

Crane-fly. Wing span 30 mm. May to September.

Robber-fly. Wing span 40 mm. July to September.

Bee-fly. Wing span 25 mm. April to May.

Hover-fly. Wing span 20 mm. April to October.

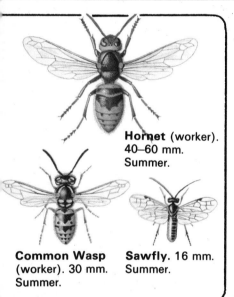

Hornet (worker). 40–60 mm. Summer.

Common Wasp (worker). 30 mm. Summer.

Sawfly. 16 mm. Summer.

Bees   (All workers)

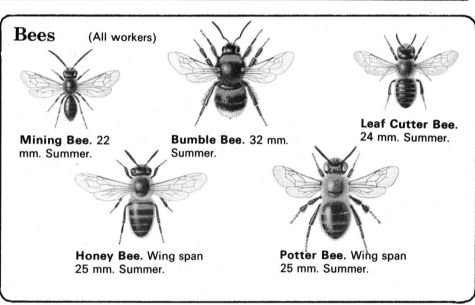

Mining Bee. 22 mm. Summer.

Bumble Bee. 32 mm. Summer.

Leaf Cutter Bee. 24 mm. Summer.

Honey Bee. Wing span 25 mm. Summer.

Potter Bee. Wing span 25 mm. Summer.

Caddis Fly

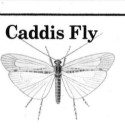

Caddis Fly. Wing span 35 mm. May to October.

Mayfly

Green Drake Mayfly. Wing span 25 mm. April to September.

Thrips

Onion Thrips. 2 mm. long. Summer.

Bristle-tails

Silverfish. 10 mm. long. All year round.

Stonefly

Stonefly. Wing span 20 mm. Summer.

Flea

Cat Flea. 2–3 mm. long. All year round.

Springtail

Water Springtail. 2 mm. long

Louse

Book Louse. 2.5 mm. long.

Index

Books to Read

A Field Guide to the Insects of Britain and Northern Europe. Michael Chinery (Collins)
The Oxford Book of Insects. John Burton (Oxford)
Insects in Colour. ed. N. D. Riley (Blandford)
Pleasure from Insects. Michael Tweedie (David and Charles)
Discovering Garden Insects. Anthony Wootton (Shire)
Studying Insects. R. L. E. Ford (Warne)
Collecting, Preserving and Studying Insects. Harold Oldroyd (Hutchinson)
Insects and Other Invertebrates in Colour. Ake Sandhall (Lutterworth)
Insects. J. Clegg (Muller)

Clubs to Join

The British Naturalists' Association (Hon. Secretary: Ms K. L. Butcher, "Willowfield", Boyneswood Road, Four Marks, Alton, Hants.) has over 20 branches in different parts of the country, and young people are welcomed on their excursions. They publish a pamphlet called *How to Begin the Study of Entomology* and others of interest to insect-watchers.
The Amateur Entomologists' Society has younger members as well as adults, who can exchange letters and news through the Society. (Prospectus from: R. D. Hilliard, 18, Golf Close, Stanmore, Middx. HA7 2PP).
The Council for Nature (address: The Zoological Gardens, Regent's Park, London NW1 4RY) is a representative body of more than 450 societies, and will supply the addresses of your local **Natural History Societies.** (Send 10p for list). Many of these have specialist sections, and almost all have field meetings. The Council will also give you the address of your local **County Naturalist Trust,** which may have a junior branch. Many of the Trusts have meetings, lectures, and opportunities for work on nature reserves.
Other useful addresses:
Natural History Museum, South Kensington, London SW7 has hundreds of insects on display.
The Nature Conservancy Council, 19/20 Belgrave Square, London SW1X 8PY.